LET IT RAIN

Tina Smith

Let It Rain

© Tina Smith

2020

All rights reserved. No part of this book may be reproduced or used in any manner without written permission of the copyright owner except for the use of quotations in a book review.

This is a work of fiction. Names, characters, and places are the product of the author's imagination or used fictitiously. Any resemblance to actual persons, living or dead, business or locales is coincidental.

Dedication

I want to Thank my Best Friend in the whole wide world, Lp Johnson, for helping me get out of my own way and freeing me at the same time. And I want to say a special thanks to my cousin-in-love Markita Hall. Both of these ladies are wonderful authors. Check them out. I also want to give a special thanks to my friends Gabi and Stephanie, for being here every step of the way. And a Special Shoutout to my sister, Chrissy !!!!

TABLE OF CONTENTS

Part One

Part Two

What's Done In The Dark

KISA

Damn! I had forgotten about that final disconnection notice from ConEd. "Please...please don't let them be here," I mutter to myself as I'm speeding up 76th and Racine street, hoping these motherfuckers didn't cut my lights off.

But when I pull slowly up to Eggleston Ave, a ConEd truck is at our two flat.

"Da-fuq? Omg *No!!*" I yell out, slapping my steering wheel in disbelief. "*Shit, shit, shit!* Oh my fucking goodness!!!"

And guess whose nosy tail out here looking up the street? Ms. Grayson. When she notices me slowly driving up to the building, she just shakes her head, looking at me. "Kisa? Kisa did you know ConEd was coming out today?" she asks, with a hit of sarcasm, raising her eyebrow at me as if to say *'with your dumbass'*.

I shoot her a *'Bitch, don't mess with me, O-kurrr?'* look. Funny looking, tired ole crow ain't got nothing else to do but bother with me. *She just mad cause my daddy doesn't want her ass no more.*

Then it hits me; Where *did* all these people come from? It was almost comical...think about it, everybody out here, watching ConEd shut my utilities off – and these the *same* folks that never saw who shot Sonny's Brother, or who robbed Mrs. Aslam, the sweetest lady on the block. But yet they all out here watching *this?* Witnessing this?

Go figure.

Getting out of my car, I pop my trunk to get my groceries out, then start walking up the street like nothing's happening (while hiding behind my bags, during my walk of shame).

Just then, the neighborhood crackhead yells out, "Aye Babe-Girl, I got that hook up on the light! I'mma come holla!"

As If we talk on the regular.

I really start to walk faster then. *Damn. This can't be happening at 9am!* Finally, I make it to my apartment, closing my eyes with a silent prayer, *Oh God, Please let these lights be on,* as I turn the key and push the door open. And...when I look at the microwave, I see the time flashing.

I'm baffled?

Just then, my cell phone rings; it's my brother, Adonis. "So...let there be light."

"Uhm...like, thank you bro. How did you know?"

"I seen your account pop up for a shut off. I...pulled a few strings... I can't have my baby sister sit in the dark, now can I? But you gotta do me a favor..."

"What's that, bro? Anything!" I say.

Adonis says, "You gotta go out with my boy, Desmond."

"Who the hell is that?" I ask.

"Sis, the dude who made your account disappear."

There I was, a grown woman, biting my nails like a fifth grader. "Uhm...okay. Okay, set it up."

"And, the beer is brewing? What took you so long to answer, Kisa? It's not like you're dating anyone."

"Really? Bro... a-ight. Talk to you later."

Thank goodness! I dodged *that* bullet! Yesss! And, *Ahhh Haaaa* to all my Fans outside!

Just then, I got a brilliant idea, about these zombies still outside. Walking to my window, I yelled out, "Ahhhhh haaaaaa! My lights on, Goofies! Go back inside! All y'all some drama queens...get a job!! Report a crime!" and put my window back down.

I'm ready for a cup of hazelnut coffee, with Caramel creamer. I could smell the aroma in the air – like, victory! -- even as I walk into my kitchen. "I can't believe I agreed to a blind date. Or did Adonis just pimp me out for $225.00?" I laughed. "Cause it's definitely gonna cost dude more! And, I'm gonna make sure the brother knows what I like, even if I don't like it! All of a sudden...*poof*...I have a taste for lobster, crab-legs, crab *cakes*, and champagne! I've been dying to go to Peaches, on 46th & King Drive. I hear their Salmon Croquettes make you want to slap your mama!" I laughed again. "Or, maybe try that other little cafe...on E. 75th...what's it called? Oh yeah, 5 Loaves Eatery." They had rave reviews about their chicken wings...but I'd heard their crab cakes were off the chain too. "I need a nap after all that. Mmm...it's been a good long while since I went out on a date. The last time was with Loe's fine self."

He was coco brown, buff, 6'2 with deep hazel brown eyes and

Dreds. I'd almost committed a crime for him! I had a thang for them 'Thugs', I didn't know why – and I knew better. Turned out, he liked THOTS; I couldn't deal with it. No more phone calls from Cook County Jail Correctional Center, burning up my phone bill. No more jailbirds.

I was also still mad as hell because he'd wanted a threesome, with me and his ex girlfriend. "Hell no! What I look like? Where they do that at? My name ain't Fifi and you are not DaPlug."

Scratching my head as I looked in the mirror, I was thinking about how long had it been since I got my nails and my hair done, not recognizing my own reflection. *I'm looking tore up from the floor up. Who **are** you?*

Dropping my robe in front of the mirror, I saw a 5.7, very attractive woman whose skin color was like sand. Thick, shoulder-length, reddish-brown hair, full, heart shaped lips; that pouty bottom lip. I loved the freckles all over my body, they looked like stars. My breasts were nice and full, 38C, though I hated the fact that my nipples were inverted. And my waist...not tiny, but just right. When I walked past the dudes on the block they said, *"There goes "Thumper',"* under their breath.

They also say my hips are screaming to carry their baby – but not me. And not with *them;* not hardly. Almost got in trouble with Loe's ass again, 6 months ago, messing around dropping moves and smoking Loud, sipping on Henny. Listening to Jeremih (*Fuck you all the time*) got me caught up. But it's no longer a problem, no more cares about it. It is what it is.

"I'm so hungry!" I realize.

Becoming a prescotarian was easier for me than becoming a full Vegan. I'd stopped eating meat a year ago, but I just couldn't shake my seafood. Other than fish though, my diet was pretty clean.

"Which reminds me...got to go to 71st & State to the fish market to pick up some red snapper and lump crabmeat. And while I'm there, I can walk to the market right up the street for some kale and collard greens, and turnip bottoms."

DESMOND

They don't get no finer, my mind is in overdrive. Foxiest woman I ever seen, Ms. Kisa Muhammad. She was at the company cookout last year, with her Dad and her brother, Adonis. I've been dying to meet her. She fine, she sexy, well put together...all that! I know her father, Mr. Muhammad...and I know he ain't having none of that, but I'm willing to take that risk if it came down to it. Anyway, it was just a dinner date.

"All that juicy ass...*ooooow!* AND her titties sitting up right." I hear myself mutter aloud.

Ah man, if she knew how many times I jerked off...starting and stopping the company DVD just to watch her ass jiggle.

"She *perfect* fa me...her skin the color of honey, sexy deep brown eyes, that thick reddish brown hair just past her shoulders. Wow! Her lips full, just the way I like...and the thought of her lips on my dick, sucking it, man...too much!"

I had to catch myself. "Ahh...like I said, it's just dinner. The only reason she's going out with me is because I wiped her account away. Other than that she wouldn't have known I ever existed."

But now I gotta figure out where to take her, was my next thought. *Damn, can't take her to Harold's Chicken, or Jerk Taco Man...or Seafood Junction. I know, I know...I'll take her to Joe Willies, on 147th & Halsted in Harvey.* "That's it. I'll take Kisa there...so cool and laid back, it'll give us time to talk and feel each other out. See where her head is."

I hope she doesn't have any kids, my mind interrupted again. *Ok even if she do, no more than two...I've had my share of crazy baby daddies and I'm good on it. Man, and I'm hoping she ain't the crazy type, loud and shit. And I hope she doesn't smoke...cause if she did it would ruin my fantasy about her. I forgot to ask Adonis if she had kids – but then he would've been like, 'What you need to know all that for? It's just a dinner date.'*

"But who knows where it could go from here?" I wondered. "Damn, I'm tripping and shit. I haven't even talked to her on the phone and already I'm on shorty like forty going north. Welp...let me go pick up my Whip...my favorite boo-thang."

I didn't like having to go through the middle man, but I understood...that was Adonis' baby sister. She was unmarried, so he was protective. But I been knowing this brother for three years, and still no invite over to the family house – or to just kick it...for more insight on Kisa...or nothing. Still, I figued he must think I'm a pretty okay kinda guy, to even allow me to talk to her, let alone take her to dinner.

"Nah, Adonis must want something," I laughed to myself. "I know him...he wants something. He could've just wiped her account himself. I was wondering why he asked me to do something he could've very well done himself. Damn, now I'm thinking what this motherfucker want..."

 And more importantly, how in the hell did he know I liked his sister? And how did he know that she would say yes? Were they setting me up? I'm young...thirty three...black, a general manager on salary here at ConEd...up for a promotion. I good got credit, don't stay with my mama, ain't got no kids, no criminal record – that they can find....even tho I did my dirt gang-banging back in the day, facts. I was never a punk...I applied that same street game to this cooperative ceiling and got down. I graduated from The University of Michigan with an MBA...yes. A career, not just a job.

 And, I got a black-on-black Audi A8 – plus, it never hurts to have that *good-good*...so I've been told. Yea, I could see how he would want his sister to date a brother like myself...I'm a hot commodity. Bad-Boy-gone-good...but you never hear about these stories in Chicago.

 I could have any girl I want, but Kisa...the icing on the cake. I want and need all that there...and I intend to land this babe. She's the cream of crop. No doubt. I hear what they're saying...this young up and coming paralegal, who's thinking about going back to school for her Law degree in family law. I like her tenacity. Smart...that's what I like, someone who can stimulate my intellect is such a turn on for me.

 I'm a little surprised at myself...I used to date 'church girls'. But some of them turned out to be some straight up hoes...straight up. To tell the truth, that's *why* me and my boys use to go to church, easy pickings! Man, we use to **live** for Sunday morning! The ladies would 'catch the Spirit' in service, and they'd be jumping up in down, dancing...titties popping out everywhere, dresses going up, panties showing –

a young boy's paradise!

Shhhid...am I wrong? I don't think so! It's like a show there, tight ass dresses, short skirts, what is it...church or the club? For real-for real.

Preacher be all dressed up, driving a brand new Cadillac to a Mega Church slapped in the middle of one of the poorest areas in Chicago. But I ain't sayin' no names. Every black block in America has one. Where's the money going to? Clearly not this area. The only thing I see is food pantries pop up all over the place – with the 'church folks' who pass out the donated food giving the poor folks in need a harder time than The Department Of Human Services, like they paid for it.

Church folks, really? You're supposed to have compassion for them, not be disrespectful towards them or stand in judgment of them. Oh how I know, I know first hand...when I was down and out, living out of my uncle's pinto on 71st & Green St. I went to the food pantry on Racine and they did ya boy Way wrong.

KISA

It's now three o'clock, seems like forever since I saw my Dad, who said he would be back here at around one o'clock to fix my cable.

"Oh my gosh," I mutter to myself, "my show, Queen Sugar, about to come on tonight. I gots to see my sexy Chocolate, Kofi Siriboe...all *kinda* yummy!"

I couldn't wait to dim the light down low, grab my favorite bottle of Stella Rosa red wine in the black bottle, get my master-blaster toy, and cum a thousand times on pause! I haven't had none since I gave some to Loe. Fuck.

Big, thick, long dick...I still shudder when I think about how he had one of my legs pinned back, he was doing me so good! Pussy was popping and purring, cumming... I need some dick, and not just any dick; some *bitch do what I say* dick...some *what's my name Bitch*...get-your-act-together-dick! *Yassssss Daddy!*

I hated myself for thinking about that negro, Loe, but I remember how he used to suck on my clit, and hold it in his mouth, and how he use to bite it. Just thinking about his monster, I wanted to cum *now.*

I turned on some porn, and there I was, stroking my pussy deeply with my master-blaster, rubbing and teasing my hard clit, shaking, about to explode. Holding my legs close together, I rolled my hips...thrusting...grinding, wishing I was in the movie with them...calling this fucker's name as the tears rolled down my face.

"You motherfucker, I hate you!"

The door bell rang...

"This can't be real."

It was my father, coming to fix the cable. I quickly jumped up, grabbing the spray and started to spray the room. But the sweet musky smell of my kitty was all in the air.

"Fuck."

So I tried spraying my Allure by Chanel, as I yell out the window that I'm on my way down to open the door. Tuning the fan on and lighting a cigarette (I stopped smoking years ago but, although every now and then I get the urge, this time I'm lighting up for a different reason), I race down the stairs to let my father in, sweating like I'm 16 again.

What the hell. I've been out of my father's house for two years now, and it still feels like yesterday to me.

As I walk back up the stairs, it dawns on me that I forgot to turn the TV off. And sure enough, my father says, in a very stern and loud voice, "Kisa, you into this type of stuff?"

"What stuff?" I say, as I scurry in the kitchen to try and play it off. Lying my ass off, to my Father of all people, I crossed my fingers behind my back. "Naw, dad...this what I was talking about. The channel keep popping up on this garbage, dad, and I'm sick of it. It's like someone has a scrambler on and is just messing up all my channels...that's why I was rushing you to come over and fix my cable." I was hoping he bought that.

Seems like he did. Dodged that bullet! Thank goodness for small miracles.

Just as fast as he got here, he was leaving.

"Thank you daddy...you're the best daddy in the whole wide world. You want to stay and have dinner with me?"

"I'm sorry, baby girl," my father answered. "I wish I could, but while I was fixing your cable, Ms. Grayson from downstairs called me and asked me to look at her garbage disposal."

Before I could say, "Dad, we don't have a garbage disposal", he was already downstairs, and she was opening the door for him and he was going in.

Thirsty butt...trying to rape my daddy! I hope my daddy tell her butt off!

But I still saw his truck out there 45 minutes later. So, I put my ear to the floorboards, listening real hard, and I could hear Mrs. Grayson laughing. There was music playing, and my father was chuckling. I haven't heard my father's laughter since Mom left and divorced him, and moved to England with her younger man. It was good to hear him laugh.

My father is still handsome, he's in his prime. Fifty-one years old, six-feet-two, and he has silver and black curly hair and piercing gray eyes. He's fit, the girls say he looks like Rick Foxx – but the Sisters at the Temple say Phillip Michael Thomas is who my Dad looks like. I gotta give it to the Sisters at the Temple, they were dead on. My dad is a dead-ringer for dude on Miami Vice. He's also a contractor with his own construction business.

"Well, the night is still young, and I got a bottle of *D'usse*."

And no one to share it with. That's a damn shame.

Just then, I felt my phone vibrate...it was my brother, sending over Desmond's number, again. He had already sent dude's number, two days ago. What would I say to him, other than thank you for helping me?

"Dammit, I should've never agreed to do this. The only reason I ever did was because I was desperate to get my lights turned back on. My brother has to be up to something!!"

Nope!! I'm not babysitting those bad ass kids so Adonis and Una can *go make **more** minions. I will not be responsible, nor will I have a part in this mayhem and madness!*

 I hoped Una had the good sense to get her tubes tied after that last set, she let Adonis trick her into thinking it would be girls. *You'd think after giving birth to her **second** set of twin boys, Una would see script:* News Flash...*don't let Adonis suck you in for the rope-a-dope again! Play close attention...my brother's first wife had a set of twin boys for Adonis too! Word on the street, my brother is looking for wife number three – wise up Una!*

 Great, now speak of the devil...and Adonis CALLS. I send bro straight to voicemail.

Let It Rain

KISA

It's raining so hard, and the thundering is so bad, it woke me up out of my sleep, nearly scaring me to death. But then my phone rings, and I see the caller I.D.

Desmond Du'Bois.

My heart skips a beat. "Hello?" I answer with fake bravery.

A strong, sexy voice responds, "Hello...Kisa? This is Desmond Du'Bois...your brother's coworker, and friend."

"Desmond...oh, yes...hello," I answer back.

"I hate to bother you at such a late hour, or sound pushy but...I was hoping it was just that, you were waiting for me to call you first."

"Yes, I was," I answer, lying through my teeth. "I thought you weren't interested...and I was way too embarrassed to tell my brother. I'm glad to know that's not the case, Desmond."

Just then, thunder hit again, and I scream, "Oh my God!"

"Kisa? Are you okay?" Desmond asked me.

"No! I'm scared of the dark, and the lights just went out! I need to go to the basement and hit the fuse box...but I don't which one that is...and Ms Grayson is out of town. My dad just left here, at ten...but he stays downtown and would have to fight through traffic."

Another boom left car alarms going off from the street.

"You know, Kisa, I wouldn't mind coming over and hitting that fuse box for you...that is if you don't mind."

"I wouldn't want to burden you with this, Desmond," I hedged.

"No trouble," he said. "Just text me your address...I stay in the 'hood too."

A wave of relief washed over my entire body. I couldn't believe Desmond was on his way over here, at this time in the morning, to flip my fuse box on. I'd lost plenty of dates in the past because I stay in a high crime area. I didn't think it was fair to judge a person purely based on their zip code – entire neighborhood profiling, shame shame shame. There were good people who stayed here too.

"Shoot...I'll be glad when he gets here, it's raining so bad I can smell the sewers backing up. I hope this basement doesn't flood. Let me get my hurricane candles...I'm so glad I put them in the fireplace and not in the storage room."

* * *

DESMOND

"Hell yea," Desmond crowed. "I'm on my way! I'm on my way to save a sexy ass damsel in distress. Hehe, thank you Lord for the thunder, lightning, and the rain to set the stage for a Bro!"

*But why is she living in one of **the** most dangerous hoods in the Chi? I'm all the way out here in Flossmoor...and she stay where I did most of my dirt...the old stomping ground. Englewood. Let me get my*

Glock, just in case some bullshit jump off and a goon come at me sideways, and I have to handle my business. You never know out here, and I would hate to get caught out. If shorty wasn't all-that I wouldn't be doing this, period...and especially out here. Hamilton Park ain't gone never change. I got into so many fist fights at the park. I use to swim out here, ball out here...I got laid out here too. All the brothers did...

Bringing back memories, good and bad. My boy Walter got shot and killed right up here at the mouth of the park, sad day that was for me and my crew. We use to call ourselves S.G.G.; Straight Gangsters Gang, cause that's what we did – straight up all day, Gangster the other gangs. We were so bad the precinct captain on 75th turned all us in, and his son was the **ringleader**. *We use to shake their asses down!*

"I see the liquor store still open...let me gab of a bottle of Moët, or Dom. Yep, they always carry this type of good stuff in the hood, cause you never know when a Baller gonna come through."

Damn, whole area out – except the liquor store. Oh yea, the only ones with a generator...gotta get that almighty Black dollar. Man, I wish black folks would band together and buy back our areas, we got stop forcing our Black business owners to sell out. **No** *black businesses on 75th, not even the one being ran by us...because the Arab man owns the whole lot, strip and all.*

I'm not hating, but we got to start educating our people. You can't go in **their** *hood and own nothing. It was a little old man who owned a barbeque place right here. Last I checked he still does, but scared to open it. Maybe I'll come back and make him a nice offer.'*

"There's her building...I was praying it wasn't this big ass building across the street. Good, a park right in front. Let me text her to let her, so I don't get my head blown off out here."

* * *

KISA

My cell phone vibrated in my pocket. "He's here!" A black Audi was pulling up as I looked out the window. Then he called.

"I'm already at the door. Come on in." I tell him. The whole area is blacked-out, so I can't make out his figure, it's too dark, only his shadow. He *sounded* sexy over the phone, and I'm hoping he's not ugly.

No ugly dudes, no more! Half of them are insecure...always asking where you at and who's that in the background. Greg Busky was a prime example, and I really liked him too; always accusing me of cheating. I couldn't deal.

And yet, a total stranger is here and the fact that I'm calm is giving me the willies.

"Ooo...there is a God..."

"How's that?" he asked as he entered.

I cleared my throat, "Thanks for coming." *No more darkness*, I hope, while we are standing in the darkness. *Calm down, you horny down cat*, I say to myself. *This man didn't come over her to lick your pussy, or fuck your brains out. You don't even know him, whore. Look at you...acting just like Mrs. Grayson's tricky ass. Every since I turned twenty-six I seem to have been losing **all** my scruples! What am I, hard up?*

Well, I haven't had a decent date in six months...my schedule is wide open on the field, and I'm available. So, hell yes, I'm anxious! I haven't had any real man contact in six months!

*As I catch myself looking into the floor-to-ceiling mirror, being full of myself, I have to ask, Looking at me...who **wouldn't** want these soft-ass lips on their hard cock...or this wet wet pussy to stick their rod into?*

I'll tell you who, Jamel's conceited self. I can't stand him. I bet he's a sexual tramp-ass. I'll never forget he left me with my panties down around my ankles, talking about he didn't know I was serious. Really, fucker?!

By Candlelight

*'Adonis didn't tell me he had an accent...Mmm, he smells so **good.**'*

My nipples started to poke a little bit and get hard.

"Where's the box?" Desmond asked.

I wanted to say, *In my pants, right here,* but Desmond was pulling out a flashlight, and now I saw the *finest,* most rugged looking man I had *ever* seen, all five foot eleven inches of him. My mouth was wide open, and I just stood there like a fool. I could hear my grandma's voice in my head, saying, *"Kisa close ya mouth before you catch a fly or something!"*

He was the color of a Heath Bar® -- the toffee part. I could see his muscles through his *Versace* shirt...and his print in his pants! My pussy instantly started getting *wet wet!* His lips were nice...

And he bowlegged...

"Kisa," Desmond called out.

"UhHmm?" I said.

"I was afraid of that," Desmond said. "I was hoping that your lights would come on, but the whole area is in blackout mode. And, it's still raining like cats and dogs out here."

Just then, a bolt of lighting hit and lit the sky up, as the thunder crackled and popped.

Desmond went on, "A crew won't be out tonight, the

weather's too dangerous."

Just then another boom lit up the sky, and I could see Desmond clearly – and *boy, oh boy* was I pleased! "Mother Nature does what she wants," I answered him back. "Well, I got plenty of hurricane candles here..."

I still had on my short-shorts, and my 'Go ahead, touch it' shirt (Doing graphic T-shirts like this is my side hustle...Hustle all day, Kisa don't play and neither do they) so I also saw the glint in his eyes as he eyeballed every curve of my body.

"Well," Desmond said, "it's raining worse over here in your area. I thought I'd grab a bottle of Moët...to break the ice. I know we hadn't planned our date just yet, but, no better time than the present."

I laughed out loud. "I guess it will be cooking in the dark for me. I know it's late...have you eaten yet, Desmond?"

"Please, call me Des," he answered. "And no, I haven't."

*With his sexy voice...up in here lookin' like Russel Wilson from the Seattle Seahawks. Yess, I wanna one-two step on him **all night**.*

"You like seafood?"

"Yes Kisa, I do," he answered.

"Good deal," I nodded. "Shrimp Fettuccine Alfredo it is. With spinach salad and a mandarin-strawberry vinaigrette...with sliced almonds, avocado, tomatoes, carrots, and croutons."

"Sounds good, Kisa. You mind if I help you?"

"Des, call me Kiki."

"I'd rather call you Kisa," Desmond said. "That way, you know I'm talking to you directly. Besides, there are way too many Kikis...*Kisa.*"

*Fuck! That just sent chills so far up my spine...**and** I like the way he says my name too. Kisa...*

"Oh, okay Des." Yep, he just scored a brownie point.

I grabbed a pot out of the cabinet under the sink and got on my step stool, to stand on the counter, on tippy toes, to grab the strainer – and I slipped. Des turned around just in time to catch me – it's *how* he caught me that got us both messed up. He caught me up by my rear end. He had his hands full of me, and my legs wrapped around him...and we locked eyes.

I immediately unwrapped my legs, sliding down him just like a stripper coming down a pole; sexy, but awkward. "Oops...thanks for catching me."

"No problem," Des said, nervously. He had the darndest look on his face, it was like someone stole his candy from him.

"Well, don't just stand there," I said. "I still need the pot."

"Yes Ma'am," Des responded. "This time I'll get the strainer too. I don't know how many times I could handle you –"

"What...falling?" Kisa interrupted him.

"No," Des interjected, "the way you did that."

"Did what?" I asked, playing dumb.

"Sliding down me the way you did."

"What?" I gave him a devilish grin. "I ain't do nothing...I got right off."

"Ight, do it again," Desmond said, "...and watch what happens. I'm not gonna let you get away so fast, slick butt."

I interrupted him again in a hurry, "Thank you for being a gentleman."

"Bet," Des said. "I'll grab the noodles, and the salt."

Finally, I get the noodles in the pot, the shrimps cleaned and de-veined, Alfredo sauce made and salad tossed.

"I got this," Des said, "I'm taking over." Then he picks me up and sets me on the counter to watch him.

"Oh?" I say.

"Allow me to bless you this morning, beautiful Lady. It's not every day this happens. I'm touched you were actually gonna cook me dinner Kisa, by candlelight."

Looking up at him, I said, "Yes...after all, you came to my aid."

Just then, Des leaned in and kissed my forehead, but then just asked, "You got any cream?"

"Yes," I responded. "Didn't you hear me say everything's in the refrigerator?"

Smirking, he answered back, "I'm gonna make you a fresh Alfredo sauce so good you will wiggle your toes."

"Okay, do that Des. Sounds good. We gonna make some butter garlic bread, too." I'm thinking to myself, *He cooks...**and** is a gentleman. I like it! Just what the doctor ordered! Everything coming together, smelling so good...*

"You wanna taste?"

"Yess..."

Des blew over the sauce. "Open your mouth for me, Kisa..."

"Oooo! This sauce taste sooo good! Yummy...I never had anything that taste this good...in a sauce."

"I told you Kisa. Now, we will incorporate the noodles in, and add the shrimp...with basil, a little salt, fresh pepper..."

The whole kitchen is smelling good now. Salad on point... The candlelight...

"I got Jiffy® biscuit mix," I tell him. "So these garlic butter biscuits will be delicious." I popped the biscuits in the oven, then walked to the buffet cabinet, to get the good China – and crystal wine glasses. I can smell the aroma of the biscuits taking me all the way home to granny's kitchen. "Skip it." I took out granny's silverware too. *What the heck, this is perfect. I never expected to have a romantic date at home in the dark candlelight!*

"Ahhh, Des? You need me to help you?"

"I got you, pretty lady."

Seeing him bring the salad in, I went to take the vinaigrette out the fridge and bring the butter to the table before going back into the kitchen. Grabbing the mitt, I opened the oven to take the biscuits out.

When Des took a call and went to the bathroom, I laughed to herself, thinking, *I hope he washes his hands...* Look at me, forever the skeptic. Here I was with this fine man who smells so good, and is being nothing but a gentleman, and I'm asking myself if he washed his hands or not. *Call me what you want to, so what.*

"Kisa..."

"Yes, Des...plates already at the table."

"Oh," he answered.

"Everything's out here...the biscuits, glasses, and dressing for the salad. All we're missing is the Fettuccine Alfredo...and you." I could see him smiling a yard wide, his face lighting up.

"If you don't mind me saying, Kisa, you are so beautiful."

"Let's wait till the lights come on," I grinned, "then see if you feel the same way."

"I have enough light to see what I like...and I like what I see." Des told me.

"I'm ready to eat, how about you Des?"

"Yes! Pass the biscuits!"

Watched him biting into that soft biscuit and licking the butter off his lips, I thought to myself, *He knows exactly what he's doing...seducing me with a biscuit. Clever...but I got Desmond... I'm about to open my mouth and suck this noodle down my throat, then lick all this good sauce off my fingers – and moan while I'm doing it too. Real...slow... I got you next time, player. Come with your A game.*

"So tell me, how often do you help damsel in distress?" *Haha, now he over there looking stuck.*

"Hardly," he answered.

"Hardly?" I challenged.

"Ight, never," Des corrected.

"What was different about this time" I asked him.

"The pretty lady I saw at the company cookout."

"Oh...last year? Really?" I was surprised. "I didn't see you there."

"Exactly why I wanted to meet you," Des answered. "I didn't want to miss my blessing again. So when your brother asked me to fix your account, I said no problem, Ms. Muhammad."

I grinned. "Let's pop this bottle of Moët...since it's just not gonna stop raining, and I'd hate to send you home in this storm."

* * *

DESMOND

*What in the hell...This girl is **full** of surprises,* Des thought to himself as he watched her grab the bottle and put her mouth over it to catch the overflow. *I don't know if she realizes what she is doing, but I hope I get the opportunity to put that mouth to the test one day.*

Shorty got me messed up if she thinks I'm about to drive all the way back to Flossmoor. She's fine and all but it's storming out here, so let me play this cool so I can land this eagle.

"Hey Kisa, you play cards?" I asked her.

"Yes Des, I do."

"Spades or Poker?"

"I play both," Kisa answered. "Lets flip a coin."

Touchdown! I grinned to myself. *Ball all day, in my court! I got that double-headed coin in my wallet that I've had since my Boy Scout days!*

"Baby girl, you about to pay...if you win we play your way, and your game. If I win my game, and my way...deal? What...? Do I sense hesitation on your part, Kisa?"

"Who me?" she gave me an innocent look. "No...I was just thinking about the ways I could make you do what I wanted you to do...torture..."

I laughed. "Really Kisa? Damn...you that confident you're gonna win? I like that in you... Um, hey, wait a minute where you going? Kisa?

"To get my lucky silver dollar piece."

I shook my head quick. "Nahhh...I'm the house-guest, you don't get to use your coin. But I got us." I pulled out the coin.

"Tails!" she called while the coin was in the air, then switched, "I mean heads!"

***

KISA

And the damn thing landed on tails.

"Aww man! Best outta three!"

"No Kisa," he had that same grin on his face. "I win...fair and square. We gone play Truth-or-Dare Strip Poker. With each hand I win, you lose an article of clothing – cause you lost the coin toss. And, you have to do a dare automatically."

"What if I win a hand?" I challenged.

"I'll take off what you want...but, I still get to dare you, cause you lost the coin toss."

"Damned if I do or don't!"

"I win!" I laughed at the end of the first hand. "So, take off your shirt."

Omg...it's better than I expected. This negro **ripped!** *Eight pack...nice. His pecks...and his chest...arms...abs... I just wanna* **lick** *him now!* Damn, I'm drooling, haha.

"I have to do a dare every hand?"

"Yes," he nodded, with his first Question. "Truth... Where is the wildest place you ever had sex?"

I answered at once, "In the camper, out back."

"Who was it?" he wanted to know.

"With my Bestie, Apple." Desmond gave me a look. "What?

We were 18 then, and experimenting."

"Did you enjoy it??

"Duh," I laughed. "I wanted to know how good pussy felt, and now I know. It I happened that one time and we're good."

Oh no, I moaned to myself when he won the next hand. "Okay, what do you want me to take off?"

"Your top," Desmond said.

I could feel my heart start to race, able to see Des staring at my tits (which were standing at attention now), biting his knuckles. *Haha, guess who's slobbering now?* I pulled the top over my head.

"Now..." he went on, playing cool. "Dare. I dare you to come over here, close to me...and let me see you play with your nipples."

As soon as I do, he grabs me and starts kissing me. I call his name softly, "Yes, Des..." as he's sucking on my lips. Rubbing his chest while kissing on his neck, I start unbuckling his belt. "Oh god," I moan passionately as I stick my hands down his pants.

His dick is so so hard. He takes my shorts off, and then takes my panties off, then he picks me up, finding his way to my bedroom even in the dark. There, he pushes me down to my knees.

"Des," I say softly. In the dark I can see his missile aimed at my mouth, so I grab it with my right hand, licking from the base all the way to the top, like a Rock Star stroking his guitar. I open my mouth and Start sucking slowly, pulling this dick to the back of my mouth, vibrating it in my throat with humming, sucking and stroking his cock.

All I hear is Des moaning in pleasure. Then he motions for me to come to him, saying he wants to look at me, and tells me what he's about to do to me. "Now, I'm gonna make you pay for teasing me with that champagne bottle earlier."

My pussy is aching so bad and is so wet I just want Des to fuck me at this point. "Be it unto me Des," I say. "Do what you will...have your way." Then I think of something. "Des..."

"Yes Kisa," he answers.

"You got protection?

"Yes."

"Okay."

He wants me to ride, so I get on top and lower myself on him, doing small circles, going down then bouncing up and slowly rolling my hips.

Then he grabs me around my waist and starts to lower me to his own rhythm, moaning as he's stroking me, pumping me, "Ahhhh ahhhhh..."

I'm moaning too as I squeeze his fat dick deep inside me, "Ahhhh...ahhh! I'm...oh Des, you feel so good!"

"You want it? Take this dick, girl, I got you Kisa. Damn this pussy so good!" Des groans. I want to let you feel everything I got..." *Damn*, he adds in his thoughts, *she so wet...my dick all in there, feeling **so** good! Let me roll her on her side so I can hit this* *pussy from the side."*

Smacking her on the ass, he watches her butt wiggle. *Ahh, that just turns me on even further.*

"Mm, Des…" I'm still calling his name, raising my legs up so he's getting all my stuff, but he flips me over and pushes my head down in the pillow and starts sticking me good…so good I scream.

"Im cummmmmmin! Des right there right there Des!"

"I'm cumming with you Kisa!" Des moans.

We both cum at the same time, and fall asleep in each other's arms.

* * *

The alarm clock is blaring.

I wake up, reach over, and…no Des.

I sit right up. It's 11am…the lights are back on. Jumping up, I hit the shower, and brush my teeth. At the same time, a million racing thoughts are going through my head. We'd polished off a whole magnum of Moët. And I didn't even remember taking shots of d'usse.

The lights are on at my house, but half the block is still out. When I walk into the kitchen I see my voicemails flashing on my phone; three missed calls from Desmond. The aroma of the coffee brings me back to life as I listen to my messages from him.

"Good Morning, Beautiful. I didn't wanna wake you up…you look like

an Angel sleeping. Thanks for dinner, drinks and the games. I really enjoyed making love to you...I hope you enjoyed me too. Talk to you soon."

Second message: *"I know I called earlier, I can't get you off my mind."*

Beep – third message: *"Kisa I'm wondering if you would go out with me again?"*

"This is so sweet." I'm moved that he's thinking about me, after sex.. on the first unofficial date. Blowing my coffee, which was still too hot, I pour a little more hazelnut creamer in it. "Ahh, just the way I like it. These giant, buttery crescent rolls with corn beef and eggs avocado are the bomb..."

Part Two

Out Of The Blue

"Hello," I answered into my cell. "Oh my goodness...Apple?" I cannot believe it! My best bestie in the world! "I've missed you! Are you back in the states? You're where? Oh, the Omni... downtown Chicago? Yes, I have a few dollars...what you trying to do? Really. Why? Okay okay, I'll bring it. And what else? Ok. hanging up now, I'll be there in two hours."

My best friend...Apple! Damn it's been a minute since I've seen cutie! She was the only one that could give me a run for the money with the boys. We used to have contests on who could pull the most dudes – she would always win.

I knew she had been having a rough time lately, though. She'd gotten married right out of college, and that one ended in a blaze of fire. And now, her second marriage was about to fall apart. Like with all her relationships in the past, some guys couldn't deal with the brains to match the beauty. Apple had graduated at the top of our class at Spellman, with a GPA that was through the roof. That was my girl, we'd been together through thick and thin. She's a 5.5, 145, and 32-22-36 knockout with long lashes, a cute nose, dimples to die for, and nice lips. Her black, thick hair has long braids that kinda put me in the mind of a black Keri Hillson – just three shades darker. That's our Apple.

"Now, I gotta go find the dope man, cause she wanna smoke some Loud and drop a move. I'm gonna get a water pipe...let me grab the rest of this drink and bring that too." To top it off, she also wanted a hoagie, from Taurus on 87 Stony Island. She had some drama to tell me. So I was going to stop at Seafood Junction too, and get two crab-leg seafood boils. "She not eating my mines up...not today or tomorrow – syke!"

I wondered what was going to happen with her and Devon? I'd never met him, but they were saying she was his equal...and if that was so, what gives with this sudden split?

"Well whatever it is, I got her back."

Taking Lake Shore Drive all the way, I finally arrived at the beautiful Omni Hotel and Suites. When I asked for her they give me her room number, and then called her to inform her I was coming up. As I get to room 130, I laugh to myself, thinking, *This bitch not gone ever change , even in her grief she keeps her goals ahead of her.* One hundred and thirty pounds is Ideal Weight in her head.

"I should've known, haha. I love this little fireball!"

* * *

APPLE

"Damn, I can't write her a letter...This my Bestie, she deserves to know why me and Devon broke up. But I don't even know where to start or how to tell her. Man, this gonna break her heart...she doesn't even suspect a thing. First though, let's get her high as hell. She's gonna hit this weed...and drink, and we gonna laugh some. Still, I better practice saying this shit in the mirror..."

Kiki...you know you my bestest best ever...but...I'm pregnant. And this baby is your brother's...

"This bitch might haul off and slap the fuck out of me, cause she gonna be wondering when-how-and-where. She gonna be looking at me real stupid – like, '*And bitch, you're married!*'

because she knows Devon is sterile... Plus she's gonna be mad at me for keeping this from her."

 She tells Adonis everything – which included how she still feels about me. Yep, that lousy motherfucker told me that...how she was struggling with her sexuality, which is some shit Adonis should've kept between brother and sister. After all, she is his twin.

 But she never said anything to me, not once...except back when we were at school, and it's been 6 years.That's the reason why I was so distant from her, I didn't want any trouble between her and Adonis.

 "But I gotta tell her. I hate this part."

* * *

KIKI

 Knocking at the door, I call out, "Apple? Apple, open the door...I've got *goodies*!"

 I put the bag down, open the door myself, and to my surprise there she is; all five foot five (one hundred and *sixty* pounds) of her, still beautiful as ever. She's sitting in the middle of the bed with the biggest container of cheese balls I had ever seen in my life.

 "APPLLLLLE!" I scream out.

 She jumps up, "KIKI!!" and we embrace one another. Then, in true Apple style, she asks, "What *took* you so long? Started to think that you had given up on me! What's in the bag?"

 "Your favorite," I answer back. "What you mean, you thought

I'd given up on you? *You* don't return calls. I've sent you emails, Kwanzaa cards... What gives, Apple?"

"Never mind about all that," she cuts me off. "For right now, let me look at you. Kiki, you're so fucking cute!"

And then she does it, the unthinkable; she grabs my face and pinches my cheeks! She *knows* I hate this!

"Girl, get over it," Apple says. "You should be used to me doing this by now...crybaby ass, get over yourself."

"Told you a thousand times that *hurts,* goofy butt."

"Okay okay, Kiki! What's in the bag?? Oh My God My Favorite!! Thank you Thank you!" She kisses me all over my face. "Come on now, Kiki...bring it in. Come on, come get this loving, girl!"

All of a sudden I'm eighteen again. I hug Apple Berry – Yea, the guys call her Apple Berry, cause she *sweet.* And I know it's true, cause we kissed that time, while grinding with our panties on, at Spellman in our dorm room. Don't judge me, people!! It was College! Everyone Was Doing It! We tried everything for the first time at school.

"What you thinking about, Ki?"

"How we gone warm up these hoagies, and our crab legs, I'm starving now."

"Yea me too, Ki. Did you get the loud?"

"Oh, that..."

"What you mean, 'oh, that',?!" Apple says in her whining-ass voice. "**That's** what I wanted! Awww Kiki!"

"Calm your goofy ass down, Apple. I got you. It's just that he was out, and as soon as he has it he's gonna bring it."

"How much did you get, Kiki?"

"A pound. I got a deal on it. I'm paying 375.00, cause I didn't know how long you were gonna be here. Plus, I still make edibles for Adonis and some of the brothers at the temple...and at the firm."

"Cool, Cool...how much you charging me, Ki?"

"Don't worry about it, I'm not charging."

"Nope. I Insist."

"Ight then, Apple, you owe me 125.00."

"Deal, I got you Kiki."

"Okay Apple. So, why you eating all these cheese balls?"

"I refuse to eat horse meat...at the burger joints...or steroid injected chicken, and microfiber particle chicken. Or that fake-ass taco meat from Taco Bell and Pepe's."

"We use to *bang* Pepe's, Apple. I still eat these bishh."

"Well you better stop, Kiki."

Oh Brother, I sigh, smirking to myself. *This health-nut will spoil a good wet dream if you let her. Wasa-crisp eatin', sesame stick chomping, water chestnut Apple-ass-head.*

"Uhm...what you say, Ki?"

"Nothing," I lie my ass off. "I was just saying let's eat."

"Damn, how many hoagies did you get, Kiki?"

"Four, and hell naw, these *ain't* all for you, greedy."

"I'm just asking!"

While we're grubbing, I mumble, "Oooow...these crab legs *good!*" And she reaches over, to take one. "Wait a minute, you better eat that hoagie!"

"*Share,* Kiki. Share! Remember, they taught us that in kindergarten. Ms. Wilson was talking about crab legs, I *assure* you! We is not about to fight over these crab legs, Kiki!"

"Apple... 'We is'?? Bad grammar coming from a Top graduate?"

"What, ever, Bish. Now pass the wine...it's too early for vodka."

Just then my cell phone rings.

"Hello? Hey Mark...you here? Ight, I'll meet you in the lobby."

Downstairs, I told him, "Mark...your payment at my house, in the mail box. I've been watching it from my new app, it's there. And, my phone will let me know as soon as you approach the house...I'll be able to see you."

"Technology something else," he nodded. "Cool."

"Thank you Mark...see you later."

"Thanks Kiki."

I start back up to the room, then, "Damn!" rush back down to the lobby. "Can I have someone bring my bags up to the room?"

"What room?" the desk clerk asks.

"130. Ms. Bishop's room."

"Yes."

"Here are the keys to the car, it's a black BMW X5. Thank you."

"Sure," the desk clerk says, as I tip her 20.00. "Gee, thanks Miss."

"You're welcome."

"What's your name?"

"Oh, my bad. Kiki Muhammad. Thank you again."

Taking the elevator back to the floor, I'm thinking, *'This Loud is **loud** as heck...omg. I wonder did they smell it?'* and laughing to myself as I walk in.

"Apple, what you doing?"

"Girl...eating these pickles and tomatoes out the hoagie, haha."

"Ookayy...to each their own..."

"Nevermind this, did you get the smoke?"

"Hell yes. Mmmm...it smells so good."

"I thought it was coming vacuum packed?"

"It did, he gave me a sample out the bag...that's what you smell."

"Pass that dope Ki..."

"You don't gotta worry, I haven't smoked since Spellman."

"Oh? So now you're Miss-goody-two-shoes?? You undercover dope smuggling, jack-legged-ass wanna-be Lawyer."

I laugh. "Dafuq? Oh, you cappin' Apple? Well damn. Ouch...that hurt. But I got you! Heavy-bottom, pear-shaped-booty having, calling-all-cars-this-One-Way ass!"

We both laughing now.

"Uhm Kiki, bisssh, don't *ever* come for me...you *still* corny with your come-back! I guess that ain't gone never change."

"Apple, all bull crap aside...you ain't come all the way out here to see me. So, what's to it?"

"Here, let me pour some wine. Why don't you get some ice?"

Lightning Bolt

"Open the door, Apple!" I yell when I get back to the room.

Her eyes get big. "Girl, where you get this big bag of ice from?"

"I ran down to the kitchen, Aye!!!"

"Let's get this party started...whoop! Turn some music on!"

I tell her, "Apple...you know, I found out that Lexi is at the Hilton, with Max. We can invite them over...it'll be like a mini reunion. Plus it will be fun!"

"Nahhh," she responds, "I'm not in the mood for people I haven't seen in years, Kiki."

"What's the matter, party animal?" I laugh, "You still holding a grudge because Max chose Lexi over you?"

"NO!!! Cut it *out,* Ki," she whines. "I just wanna spend some time with my bestie... Okay bestie?"

"Aw, that's so sweet, Apple! Aww...bring it in, bring it in..."

"No, Kiki...seriously. I mean it."

She was serious too. "*Okay.* Damn. You ultra sensitive. Ight then, what is it? You don't want them to know you get high? If that's it, I get it."

"Yeah, that's it Kiki. Just wanna let my hair down."

"Okay friend, it's whatever." I switched it up. "Welp, I might as well break out what I got for you."

 Her eyes lit up at that. "You got me something, Kiki? You shouldn't have!"

 "Let me run back to this room and pull it out of my suitcase...close your eyes!" I said, hurrying to the back. "Ta Daaaaa! Open your eyes."

 "Awww, Kiki...this is beautiful! The most beautiful bong I've ever seen. What's that, at the base...?"

 "Jade and jasper, entwined together...and it's all crystal."

 "Awww, come here Kiki...bring it in..."

 "Bringing it in..."

 She laughed suddenly, holding it up. "Girl bye. Haha. Shiddd, I'm pouring some Henny in here."

 "You got Henny here, Apple?"

 "Yes Kiki. And, your ass gone hit this with me!"

 "Omg Apple."

 "Bissh...you hitting this when I light up! Oow! *No Guidance!* (by Chris Brown & Drake) This my song...turn that up, Kiki!"

 "You got it, Girl!"

 "Girl...Bang that! Damn! I can feel the music vibration all over me!"

 "That's that weed, Apple, haha. I'm feeling good too.

"Come get this drink, girl." She's holding the Henny. I shake my head.

"I'm still sippin' the cup I had from earlier…"

Apple ain't even trying to hear it. She moves over to me. "Uhm uhm, ok bitch…come here, hold your head back."

"Stop, Apple."

"Bitch relax. Open your mouth wide and swallow…like Loe used to tell you to."

"Don't drown me, hoe."

"Swallow bitch."

"Ahhh!" I gasp after a coughing fit. "Damn trick, you just tried to kill me!"

Apple was laughing uncontrollably. "Ooow Ki, you should see your *face*…it's super red!"

I wasn't laughing.

Apple didn't care. "Hey Kiki…next time leave *Kisa* bitch-ass at home. Now calm your stuck-up tail down."

And just like that, I'm high off the Henny, laughing at stupid shit that doesn't make any sense.

"Heyyyy Kiki, your eyes red as heck too, hahahaha!" She grabs the bong. "Come on, let's smoke…please Kiki, please?"

"Okay okay! One time, that's it."

"Okay. Pinky Promise."

"Nahhhh. I don't wanna."

"Kiki, come on!" Apple screams out." You can't take it back! Come on now, Ki. Let's dance. Turn up."

"Okay...put that disc on track 2 and let it play out."

"What is this, a hot mix?"

"Yes Apple."

"Ooow, it's beautiful! It lights up too? Cool!" Apple put a nice piece of loud in the bowl. "This smell so good!" She turns the torch up and pulls.

"Wait, ain't nothing at the bottom of the bong." I pass Apple the Henny. "Now hit it."

 Apple takes a long toke and blows the smoke in my face. "Helllllll Yeaaaaaa!" Apple hits it again and falls back. "Oooow shiiiiiii, Ki!!!! Come on, I got you Ki, I promise. I'm not gonna let nothing happen to you."

"Okay...you know I'm scared,"

"Don't worry, I got you."

I take a good, long drag – with my dumbass, knowing how long it's been since I smoked.

"Whoa! Whoa Kiki!" she laughs. "Pull *slowly!*"

"Mmmm...Apple..."

Apple puts some more in the bowl. "I got you, Ki. This second one – "

"No No No, that first hit messed me up, Apple."

"Ight Ight...I'll give you a shotgun."

"Am I gonna be alright, Apple?" I ask her.

"Shut up. You extra, Ki. I said I *got* you. I'm gonna put a little more in the bowl so we can both get a good one, and then we gonna chill and talk, okay?"

I watch as Apple puts a real good one in the bowl and lights up.

"C'mere Ki, get closer to my mouth." Apple blows smoke in my mouth.

"Mmmm this is good."

"Uhm Kiki."

"I'm high as heck, Apple."

"Not yet, Kiki. Come on, we having fun, loosen up. Here, take a shot. Now Imma take one. Come on, this last one. Imma set up one last time."

I press my lips up to Apple's one last time while she blows. "Hold your nose on this one Kiki."

It went straight to my head. "Omg." Suddenly the room was spinning. "Whoa!"

"You good, Ki?" asks Apple. I nod without speaking. "Okay

Ki... I'm high too. How you feel? Good?"

"Yes..." I mumble, then laugh, "Haha, look at your nose, Apple...it's...it's..."

"It's what, Kiki?"

"It's moving! Hahahaha! Oooo...Apple..."

"What?"

"Why you let me get high like this?"

"I got something to tell you."

I knew it had to be something. "Tell me."

"Wait, first let me give you what I got to give you, Okay?" she stalls. "And then Imma tell you. Close your eyes."

"Should I hold my hands out?"

"Yes."

"Okay. I'm so excited!"

"I'm coming...keep your eyes closed!" I hear her 'sneak' back into the room. "Open your eyes."

When I do, the lights are off, but I can see Apple standing there, butt naked. "Apple...what's going on?"

"I wanna have some fun, Kiki. I wanna fuck...and I want you to fuck with me too."

"Apple..."

"Shut up Kiki. I know you want this."

And just like that, Apple grabs me and kisses me deeply. "Mmm...Kiki kiss me back. We never finished that day...the last day I was here. And I've been thinking about it, Kiki."

"That was your fault, Apple." But I'm kissing her back.

Apple starts to take my shirt off, as we start French kissing. Then I'm kissing all over her neck, and all over her stomach.

"Kiki mmmm...Kiki I'm so hot, please lick me." I suck her nipples, biting them. "Ahhhh....ahhhh!" Apple moans out as I'm licking my tongue all across her nipples and sucking them. When she screams again, I reach back up to squeeze her titties.

"I missed you, Apple." Rubbing her ass, I part her legs. "Are you sure you want me to do this?" I ask her, to be sure myself. As soon as she nods her head, yes, I start sucking on her clit, flicking my tongue in rings around and across it, and sticking my tongue deep inside her pussy.

She's screaming, "*Ki!*" and pushing my head closer, so I stick my tongue inside her pussy again, and fuck her with my fingers, sticking two inside her now, while I'm rubbing her clit.

"Kiki! Please! I want to cum!" she begs me.

"Bitch, scoot back." She must be crazy if she thinks I'm not going to get some pussy. I get her in a scissor position. "Ooow yes, this shit feels so good." I'm caught up, pumping and rubbing, then I start choking her.

"Kiki!" Apple calls my name.

"Bitch move your ass," I tell her. So she starts moving. "Mmm, yes Apple."

We're both enjoying ourselves, rubbing and bumping and, just when we're cumming, she's suddenly crying, so I start sucking her clit again, until she screams, "Kiki! Kiki!"

And that's when Apple tells me. *While we're cumming!* This Crazy Nut tells me she been having affair with my twin brother...and she's pregnant?!

"WTF?!" I'd slapped the fuck out of her before I knew it. "I'm sorry, Apple, I'm leaving."

"No Kiki!" she stops me. "Th-There's s-something else."

"Really?" If looks could kill she'd explode right now. "Like What?"

"Adonis doesn't know I'm pregnant," she whines.

"Man...Apple, *Fuck* Adonis Man!" I yell at her. Then I think of something else. "How long, Apple?"

"Kiki..."

"Mannnn...*how long* you been fucking him?! I bet you didn't even tell him we were planning to hook up every other 90 days. And every Kwanza. **Did** you Apple? Did you?"

"No."

"Yea, I was wondering what happened to your ass. How could you fuck my brother and fuck me too, Apple? **What** was you trying to do?" I went on before she could answer. "The deal was, you stay married to this broke dick motherfucker. But you let *Adonis* fuck you...***and*** get you pregnant?! I can't **believe** you!"

"Ki!!!! Ki!!!!"

I gave her a look. "Yea. You knew what you were doing...you got me high so I wouldn't respond fucked up, cause you knew I'd beat your ass all through here! Let me go."

"Kiki, babe...please," Apple tried again.

"Don't 'baby please' me, bitch! You are *incredible!*" I came back to my first question, "**How long** have you and this dirty motherfucker been laughing at me?!"

"Kiiiii!!!" Apple cried. "He doesn't know about Us!"

"WHY, Apple? Why wouldn't you tell my brother that you're in love with me? Or about how you ruined my last relationship, just four months ago, after you disappeared?" Tears are streaming down my face. Then the light came on, making me even more pissed. "Is *that* when you started fucking him? How many months are you?"

"Kiki..."

"HOW MANY MONTHS, Apple??"

"Four," she admitted.

"Yeap! I *knew* it, you selfish bitch."

"Kiki, don't cry...please babe..."

"Bitch, I just told you to let me go, Apple."

"No, Kiki, I'm not letting you drive under the influence, and you're hurt and angry."

I wasn't trying to hear it, and we end up fighting.

Apple finally got my keys, telling me, "Backup Kiki...before I throw these motherfucking keys out the window."

I turn away for a sip of my drink, and end up downing all of it. Then, moving quick, I grab her, slam her into the bed, pushing her head down into the pillow, and I start to choke her again. But just then, I catch myself in the mirror, choking my friend – and, she's pregnant.

"What the fuck am I doing?? Apple? Bae, you alright?" I grab her and start kissing her. "I'm so sorry." I wipe her tears away, but then turn away again.

"Kiki...where you going?"

"For a walk. I need some air...I can't deal."

Tears are streaming down Apple's face as she comes chasing behind me, her hair sticking up all over her head, makeup everywhere.

"Ki...come back! You in your panties and T-shirt!"

"What?" I snap out of my daze, but something else dawns on me. "Apple, what you put in my drink?"

"Aww Kiki..." she whines, acting hurt.

"Everything fuzzy..."

 She finally admits, "Bitch, a sleeping pill. You was tripping the fuck out! Now calm your ass *all* the way down."

 I still storm out of the room. But that quick, three doors away, I'm passed out in the hallway.

 People soon started looking at us, and I think I heard Apple telling them I had a seizure. I was barely awake, but I heard somebody say, "Should we call EMS, ma'am?" And I could hear this hoe saying, "Nah, she good." And I'm thinking to myself, *This the mother that poisoned me. I'm all outside my body...somebody help me...*

Disaster

My head is *pounding*, and the alarm clock is blaring. And my messages are beeping too.

"Eeeek! Aaaaaah, can the world just stop and let me get off!! Who in the world opened the curtains?" I grumbled, but then realized where I was. "How did I get home?"

But now, I can smell the aroma of coffee from the kitchen. "Who's in the kitchen?! Shhhh..." I slowly get up, cautiously, and tiptoe to peek out. And I see...

"Awwww, nah! Hellll Nah! *Loe?*!!"

"G'morning Kiki. Bae, I need to talk to you about what you were doing last night. Here..." Loe hands me the coffee. "Kiki, ain't no time for you to be looking all fucking confused and shit, cause you were clowning last night."

"Loe, Please. I got a headache. How did I get home? And why are you here?"

"Apple Berry called me and told me you had a seizer, but I'm not stupid, Kiki you were plastered out your mind. And so you know I saw what was in your purse."

I turned all the way around to look at him. "I...I was taking them to stay awake."

"Kiki who do you think you're talking to?" Loe says. "I *know* you, Kiki. You might be able to trick all these other dummies at the office and around here, but I know the game. And...who the fuck is Desmond? Ol hoe-ass name for nigga."

"It's none of *your* business, Loe," I tell him.

"Oh? So you want me to call your Daddy and tell *him* that I found you naked in a hotel room, crying, and talking about our baby you lost? Huh, Kiki? Does he even know?" My face gave the answer. "You still didn't tell him. "

"Loe, uhm, sorry," I backtrack.

"Shut the fuck up, Kiki. Don't 'Loe I'm sorry' me. This just why I'm not with your ass...all the rules, and fucking secret-girl...you need to stop it, for real."

"Ohhhh, my head," I turn away, walking to the bathroom to get the aspirin out the medicine cabinet. "Okay Loe, I got it now. Thank you, for everything, really." I tell him, as I walk back to the kitchen.

"Hey, Kiki, you know you cried all night...about the baby. How come you didn't tell me you were still hurting about this?"

"Yea, I musta really been doped up..." I mumble, mostly to myself. To him, I answer back, "Must have been some suppressed feelings I was harboring."

"Kiki, I asked you to go to therapy with me, but you just wanted to act like our son never existed. And poor Apple...that's supposed to be your best friend. You never even told her you were pregnant a year ago."

"Loe, that was family business...our personal business."

"You don't answer my calls, or answer my text messages. Our son was *real,* Bae. He lived for 24 hours. And Kiki, Lj's Birthday is coming…do you even remember his birthday?”

“*What do you **want** from me, Loe*?!” I scream out finally. “Of course I know his birthday is coming up! That was a low blow, even for you, Loe!” I looked up at him with tears in my eyes. “How could you say this to me?”

“Kiki, you were stoned *giving birth*!”

“I'm so **done** with you, Loe! Get out!! Get the hell out of my house!!”

“Glad to, you Baby-killer bitch!”

“YOU SON-OF-A-BITCH!!!” I snarled at him. “I HAD A SEIZURE! I got slammed to the ground while getting *robbed*, and went into Labor! You rotten MOTHERFUCKER! They gave me medicine…so…I…would stop…seizing. Oh God…you blame *me* for Lj's death!”

“You were *high*, too. I saw the toxicology report, Kiki. And I hold you directly responsible for not taking care of yourself during the first five months you were pregnant.”

“Loe, you were right there with me! I did everything I was supposed to do. That's not fair!”

“Kiki…don't make me tell you what's not ‘fair’.”

“Loe, will you please leave me –”

“No!” Loe grabbed me and made me look at him. “Kiki *look* at you! Still stoned! Look at yourself in the mirror, for once, *face* yourself!”

I look, with tears streaming down my face. My lips are as dry as sand, hair sticking to my scalp, blood on my shirt... "How did this blood – whose blood is this?"

"Yours, Kiki. I told you...you were acting a *fool*. I had to restrain you. You bit me so hard, I went to jerk away my arm and you got hit in the nose somehow. I held you all night long, while you begged me to take your pain away. You said, 'make you feel good'...but you know I like it sober. I want you coherent when I'm putting it down, especially with you. And for the record, Kiki, no...I didn't tap that ass while you were out of it – though I should've."

"Loe, you can let yourself out," I came back, not responding to any of that. "I'm hopping in the shower. On second thought, here...I'll walk you to the door."

Loe reached to lift my chin up. "Baby girl, I'm sorry for what I said earlier to you. Me and you gone always be family...and when you done acting a fool, I got something for you."

* * *

"Hey Des. This is KIki, so sorry that I missed your call. I got tied up after work...had some deadlines I had to meet. I want you to know that I had a wonderful time as well, and I look forward to going out with you again...this time we will make reservations, haha. And make sure the weather is good. I'll call you when I make it home this evening."

Finally, I get to relax for a moment. No phones ringing, no notification alarm sounds going off, just sweet peace.

Then my phone rings.

"Kisa, how are you?"

"Hello Desmond...I was just about to answer the phone but you were hanging up."

"You busy, Kisa?"

"No, no...not at all. As a matter of fact, I was just thinking about our time together."

"Is that right?" Des smirked to himself.

"Uhmm."

"What are you doing now, beautiful lady?"

"I. uh...whelp, nothing. Haha. Just drying my hair. What's up, Des? Ah...hold on a minute, someone's at the door."

Looking out the window I see an FDS floral truck outside. When get down to the door, I look through the peephole and see the delivery person. I open up the door and I say, "There must be some kinda mistake."

"Delivery for...Kisa Muhammad?"

"I'm Kisa." I confirm, confused.

"Then, these are for you."

I'm standing there in shock, mouth wide open. Walking back into my two flat Graystone building and ascending the stairs, I open the door, still staring at this beautiful arrangement of gardenia, peonies, and tea roses.

Just then, I remembered I was on the phone. "Oh! Desmond, Um...so-sorry. I just got a delivery. Of flowers.

"Who are they from?" Desmond asks in an oh-so-surprised voice. "Did you read the card?"

Card? No. What card? This was the first time I'd ever received flowers – but I couldn't say that out loud, like, he can't know this. So, I resort to the next-best thing and say, "Oh, Yea."

Then: "Desmond! Oh my goodness, these are *so* beautiful! *Thank* you! Ooh I just wanna hug you for...this is the nicest gesture I've received in a while."

Desmond came back, "I just happened to be in the neighborhood...right up the street. Since you wanna hug a brother, I don't want to miss out...be it far from me that I should ever disappoint you. Never. I'd like to collect that Hug. That is, if you don't mind?"

I look out the window again, and seeing Desmond pulling up gave me butterflies. *Wow, Desmond got me blushing like a freshman in college.* Just then I was transported back to that stormy night, and the way he smelled. *Damn Damn...ahhh. This fine ass brother's about to step out his whip and see me. Yea, come get this hug.*

"And whatever else he wants."

There he was, looking like a quarter-link. A well-dressed, sexy black man in a pullover baby blue Ralph Lauren cashmere sweater, with Gucci jeans on over his caramel-colored, ostrich-skin cowboy boots. I was loving it, every sexy moment of it.

And here I am, standing here with a terry-cloth robe on, and mismatched panty & bra underneath it. I shook my head at myself.

"Hey Kisa."

"Hey Des."

"Good morning, beautiful lady. I'm here for that hug."

"Come in...want some tea, Des?"

"I know this is last minute, Kisa, but I'm hoping I can take you to Brunch? I hear the House Of Blues has a wonderful Sunday brunch."
"I've heard it's out of sight, Des. I would love to go. Where is it located?"

"226 N. Dearborn...it starts at 11:30."

"Say no more. I was just about to get dressed when you called. I'll be ready in 15 minutes."

I went quickly to my closet, thankful that I had a brand new Prada dress. It's cream colored, and will complement what he's wearing perfectly. I also have a baby-blue, sapphire earrings/bracelet/ring and necklace set.

"Let's see," I mutter under my breath. "My nude Prada platform shoes...baby blue LV clutch...looking good. I'm just gonna put my hair in a high bun, and let some ringlet curls fall loosely from the sides...yeah. And...a spray of my flower bomb perfume."

As I walk out of my room I can hear Desmond having a very serious conversation on the phone, so I clear my throat, just to let him know that I'm approaching.

"You...you look so scrumptious. Can I say that?"

"You may, most kind Sir. Is everything okay, Des?"

"Oh, yessss...why wouldn't it be?"

"I, I kinda heard your voice rise to an octave that most men reach in anger."

"Oh that? Ahh, nothing to worry your pretty head about. You ready?"

"Yes Des."

And just like that we were on our way to the House of Blues.

3 hours later

Damn, who keeps blowing me up? 3 missed calls from Loe...hm, I wonder what he wants. Probably nothing, screw him. Aww, it's almost over. Dang.

"Here we are, pretty lady," Desmond said as he pulled up to the graystone.

"Why don't you come in for afternoon cocktail, Des?"

"Ight," he agreed.

"Oh my God," I whine, my looking through my purse like a mad woman for my keys. "Fuckkkkk!" Finally, I reach up for my spare keys over the door. Inside, I tell Des, "Come sit next to me. What? You scared now? Haha, just kidding."

"Nah, I ain't never scared," Desmond responded, grinning.

"White wine okay?"

"Yes it is."

"Pour us up then, Des."

He pours while I kick off my shoes. "A toast, to us," he held up his glass. "Here's to a long and meaningful friendship."

"Here, here. Oooow...my tootsies hurt." I notice.

Desmond tapped his leg, motioning for me to put my feet up on him. "I give the greatest foot massages ever," he said.

"I'll be the judge of that," I say back to him. But I put my feet up. "Mmmmmm, this *does* feel so good." I lean towards him, and our lips lock. Des kisses me passionately, until I move to jump in his lap.

Just then, the front door opens, and Loe enters.

"What the fuck?" he growls when he sees me in Desmond's lap.

"Damn," Des moves me so he can get up. "Why didn't you tell me you were dating? If I would've known you had another nigga, I wouldn't have come." He paused for a second, then Loe realized who he had to be.

"Oh...so this nigga Desmond?"

"Oh, slow ya roll boy," I interrupt.

But Des interrupts me, "What you know about me?"

"What don't I know about you, hoe ass nigga?"

"Loe!!!" I yell. "Stop it! Stop it Des! Stop it stop it, he doesn't know anything about you. Please Stop! Stop!" I try to jump in between them, and get knocked to the floor as they square up. So, I do the next best thing. Scrambling to the front room, I grab my gun.

"YO!! Put the gun away!" Loe squeaks.

But it's too late, two shotgun blasts are already leaving the gun. I just scream.

Five minutes later, Sirens are blaring, my cell phone is ringing, and noises are coming up from people down on the street, screaming, "Kiki are you alright?!!?"

About 30 cop cars quickly surround the building, trying to assess the situation.

As the shock wears off, both Loe and Des say in unison;

"WHAT THE FUCK!!! Are you *crazy* Kiki?!"

"What the fuck!!!! Bitch!!!! You done let off shotgun blasts in this part of the hood!"

"COME OUT WITH YOUR HANDS UP!!!!" we hear the Cop say on the bullhorn.

"How we gone get out of this??" Desmond complains. "Fuck."

ABOUT THE AUTHOR

Author Tina Smith is a native of Chicago who lives with her husband and their two children. When she's not writing she enjoys focusing on her bead crafts and her work as a professional caretaker.

Coming Soon

There's A Storm a-Comin'